1

U.J.Garland

A KILLER RIDE

Story by J.R.Prosser

Reimagined & Written.

By V.J.Garland

U.J.Garland

A Killer Ride by V.J.Garland

Original Story by J.R.Prosser

Published by V.J.Garland

https://vanessajgarland.godaddysites.com/

Copyright © 2021 V.J.Garland

For permissions contact: vgarland89@outlook.com

Book Cover by Henry Hession

Models: Hunter Karpati & Henry Hession

Page Imagery Credit to Kevin Dooley:
https://www.flickr.com/photos/pagedooley/

ISBN: 13 978-0-6487069-3-9

First Edition.

Genre: Thriller/Horror

Summary: Clint and Wade have pretty simple MO's. Clint kills hitchhikers and Wade is a hitchhiker who kills those who pick him up. A chance meeting between the two puts them in the car together. Will Clint fall victim to Wade? Or will Wade be another notch in Clint's belt?

SPECIAL THANKS FROM THE AUTHOR

A big thank you to all my family and friends for continually supporting my literary ventures.

U. J. Garland

U. J. Garland

6

SPECIAL THANKS FROM THE CONTRIBUTOR

SPECIAL THANKS TO MY FAMILY AND
FRIENDS FOR SUPPORTING THIS BOOK
IDEA, AND THE BIGGEST THANKS TO
THE AUTHOR, VJ GARLAND, FOR
MAKING THIS DREAM COME TRUE, IT'S
NOTHING WITHOUT HER.

GO DAWGS!

A
KILLER
RIDE

WADE

The sky filled with its dusty red hue as the sun began to rise over the hills. I slipped out the back of the house through the same broken window I'd smashed earlier in a vicious rage. The body dangled, still draining of blood. The spine ripping slowly from the weight of the woman who hung from the cloak hook. A pool of blood expanding as it seeped out from underneath the front door down the porch.

The scent drew in a wild cougar, and I listened in awe as the wild cat scraped at the wooden door, desperate to chow on my latest kill.

She had picked me up at a supermarket, typical do-gooder, her first mistake was assuming I was homeless, her second presuming she could clean me up and fix me a meal. She'd played with my oily shoulder-length hair on the way back to her house.

I don't know what pissed me off more, the overbearing mothering or the putrid scent of lavender that enveloped her wagon. I wasn't sure by the time we arrived if she wanted to mother me or fuck me. She was easily 10 years my senior.

Sirens wailed as animal control rolled up to the home and the cougar ran off leaving footprints of blood. I was too close for comfort; I'd lingered too long.

Patrol cars showed up next forcing entry into the home. I'd barely escaped and raced down the highway, sirens wailed immediately as I hurried in the opposite direction on foot. Ambulances and more police rolled down the street still in eyesight towards the scene of the crime.

I made my best attempts to hail cars down, all passing me by, some slowing to take a closer look at me, but then quickly speeding off as they observed my scruffy beard and rancid clothing. It'd have been a sensible idea to steal some clothes from Miss Goody, but I was too immersed in watching her leak biofluid all over the floorboards, I didn't mean blood. It was amusing to me to watch how a body would naturally evacuate the bowels once fear set in. She'd had some pretty terrible Mexican by the smell of it, but I still couldn't tear my eyes nor nose away. I'd sat intrigued as I observed her body enter livor mortis.

Purple coloration set in, and algor was slowly brewing when the first siren invaded my euphoria.

The putrid stench had become exhilarating to me, like catnip to a cat, or anise to a dog. It was the smell of a successful kill, and my only desire was to revel in it.

The road was barely dark now, highway lights began to flicker before they held their buzzing burn ready to sign off for the night as light began to skip in over the hills. Cars became fewer and the red and blue beams were dulling as I dragged myself further down the dirt beside the road, it was quieter now, peak hour traffic had subsided.

The offensively loud roaring of an obnoxious engine could be heard well before the Gran Torino in hunter green with silver stripes paused in front of me. A solid man rolled down the window, black buzzed hair with Neil Sedaka blasting on the sound system. He sure was a fool, just like old Carol's lover.

"The names Clint," He grunted in a husky tone to match his brawly stature.

"Wade," I chimed.

"Where you headed, pal?" Clint queried.

"Anywhere..." I was exasperated. I let out a deep breath as I eagerly jumped into the car.

Clint snickered and blared the music louder. His taste was questionable, Louis Armstrong was next to offend my ears. Then Barbra Streisand.

"Old soul?" I asked cheekily ready to prime him for my next kill.

"You don't appreciate the golden oldies do you, pal?" he chuffed.

"I'm more into ambiance, rain, dripping," I meant the dripping of blood, the sound of it on a tin roof isn't like rain hitting it, it was a different consistency, its crash was more violent and thrilling, the tiny splatters that followed, it never ceased to amaze me how far one small drop could splatter, I felt the goosebumps bound over my skin as the excitement burst through me at the thought of it.

My focus was blurry, it was hard to concentrate on conversing, especially with a dim-witted hot head. He raced through the desert for hours. The guy tried to soften the mood, he even turned off his music and started cracking jokes and making weird small talk.

"Most folk who come this far out into the desert don't go back," he chuckled.

"Sounds like you do?" I peered at him.

"Gotta play your cards right, pal," he cackled wildly.

14

I squared him off and diverted my attention out the window as the blinded me into squeezing my eyes shut.

It was nothing but mounds of rock, cactuses, and the odd set of bright eyes running in the opposite direction, I had no idea where I was, I didn't care.

The music was beaming as if he was turning it louder every so often like a sneaky child. I'd had enough of this old era for one night. We were about 3 hours into the desert when I flicked the station from white noise to more white noise, but I finally came across a rock station that occasionally blinked out. Clint glared at me but seemed to allow it. ACDC seemed to be the band of choice and once in a while, I'd catch a smirk as Clint seemed to enjoy the music.

"You're a rocker?" he questioned as he bopped along to 'Back in Black'.

"Absolutely!" I said with wide eyes.

Rock was the best kind of music to accompany a good slaying, even a clean-up when the mood struck, which it hadn't for months. It was the chase that drew me, the adrenaline, it was exciting to evade a scene right as cops were showing up, I always stayed till the very last minute. A teasing lick of my scent still pondering in the air, and then I'd vanish. This was my sex and I craved it like a dog in heat.

The chatter between us was bleak, tolerated at best and I couldn't wait to see where we pulled up for the night and unravel how I'd butcher this moron. He had a nice car, I'd planned on taking it for a ride further north, maybe Sedona. There'd be a good amount of slutty bodies and jacked-up beef heads laying around Havasu Falls. I could make that flow red.

Music banged on in the background and Clint was immersed in the drive. His eyes were heavy, but serious. They had a tinge of fire in them, a man on a mission. I hadn't bothered asking exactly where we were heading. We were never going to arrive, so I didn't see the point in investing my breath in that conversation.

I was getting itchy for more action, but I couldn't knock off this guy just yet, we were approaching a lot of stores and even though it wasn't my regular style I was hungry for that fix, I'd been interrupted by that damn cougar with Miss Goody far too soon.

It might not be a do-good-er, but I bet I could find some good juice in that store just waiting for the opportunity to throw me a pity stare. That's all it took, that was why I zoned in on those willing to give me a ride. They carried too much empathy, I thrived on that.

I began to think it might be damn well worthwhile and deeply exciting to explore this another way.

DETECTIVE WESTWOOD

I was the first car on the scene, the second murder in a week. Bloody paw prints painted the front porch like a puzzle to be followed, scratch marks clawed deeply into the front door as the animal had hungrily tried to make the most of the situation.

I had two of the younger police officers kick the door in. We were immediately engulfed with the wrenching stench of human shit. It took less than a heartbeat for these young bucks to be out on the porch chundering their guts up over the bushes.

I braced myself and entered the room trying carefully not to step in the blood. The body was to my right, strung up from a cloak hook, the weight clearly too much as the screws slowly pulled away from the wall.

"Let's get a bag in here! Gotta move fast everybody!" I shouted to the Medics and EMS.

Fire and Rescue were at the scene. Once forensics had photos the body was removed, samples were taken and the everlasting hunt for the remaining body parts begun. I knew this woman, she was my sons' third-grade teacher, also known as the town hussy. She'd been scalped, had several of her fake nails ripped from their beds and a canine tooth pulled, broken gum hanging out from her mouth. Feces stained her skirt and legs; it was as if the scent of the blood intensified the odor of her excretion.

Hernandez tripped through the door still zipping his fly.

"Late..." I scowled as I acknowledged his sloppiness.

"Sorry, Westwood. I just got the call as I was leaving the gym," he claimed.

Every first responder here knew he was shagging the fire chief's daughter. He was younger than me, young for a detective, mid-'30s, and still acted like a complete jock. I was 10 years his senior and he never let me forget it. As long as he wasn't shagging my daughter I could care less, but his carelessness was becoming a pain. I couldn't keep rocking up to scenes like this alone.

"You should have been here an hour ago, what if the perp was inside?" I shouted.

His head sunk as the entire street and teams heard my deep voice rage right through him.

"It won't happen again," He sighed.

"You're damn right it won't, or you'll be pushing papers and issuing parking tickets for the rest of your career," I growled in my husky faint voice.

His brows furrowed as beads of sweat cascaded down his cheeks.

"Where's the body?" he questioned as he walked about the house.

"It's already gone," I glared as he paced the wooden floorboards.

"Oh," he whimpered.

"Don't make me make an example out of you Diego, you're a good detective but pussy clouds your brain, I can't rely on you," I explained trying to cut him some slack now that we were out of sight and earshot from others.

"Isn't she a little young for you?" I questioned.

"24, if the chief finds out he'll have the whole firehouse throw me in the next blaze," He sighed.

"Lucky for you it's fall," I joked.

Callie was my kid's babysitter when they were in junior high. She was well known and well-liked in our small town of Tempe. Diego was mad about her, but she was in and out of town for college. That's when he lost focus, when she came home.

"You either man up and tell the chief you want to marry that girl, or you leave her alone," I snuffed.

"Marry?" he scoffed.

"That's what you do when you grow up Hernandez," I chuckled.

"I still feel like I'm a kid some days," he confessed. His goofy face lighting up.

"Well, kids don't belong on my crime scenes..." I glared.

He was looking over walls with a blacklight torch and the wall facing the hooks had snags of long brown hair. The victim was platinum blonde.

"I think you found something!' I chimed.

Diego's jaw dropped as he moved in closer to the evidence.

"Get the evidence kit," I ordered.

He raced out to the vehicle almost tripping over his own feet as he stumbled out the door. He was a bright guy, extremely intelligent, but a complete klutz. An accident on legs. You wouldn't guess it by looking at him, he was tall, 6'3, brown side-swept hair, well presented with a lean but muscular build.

He wrestled the kit through the front door trying not to knock over the forensics team.

"That's the rape kit, you knucklehead!" I grunted as he handed me the black bag.

"Ahh, shit!" he muttered.

"I'll get it myself..." I grunted as I pushed past him.

The coroner was outside with the body, a few other patrol cars, and EMT'S. The house was being gutted for evidence and the FBI was beginning to roll in. I grabbed the evidence kit and dragged it inside.

"Head's up, FBI just rolled in. Compose yourself," I smacked Diego on the back.

You could see the nerves rattling his whole stature. His breaths were long and deep as he tried to control the shaking of his hands while he tweezed the hair from the wall. He placed it in the clear tube and moved onto swabs of blood.

He was trying desperately to stay focused, but the sweat was pooling on his forehead.

"Hernandez, don't let that drip…" I said handing him a towelette.

"Thanks, Boss," he smiled up at me.

"You know I'm only tough on you because I see so much potential," I said trying to soften the ambiance between us.

"I know, Westwood. My brains just scrambled, I'll do better," he promised with a sigh.

"Westwood, the MO lines up with the previous victim. Same guy, and messy as ever," said the FBI agent as he held up the tube with the hair in it.

"And what does MO stand for Hernandez?" asked the agent in a harsh serious tone.

"Ahhh… Modus Operandi, Sir," he gleamed.

"He's a bright bugger, I didn't even know that!" he laughed as Diego let out a deep breath.

"We just like to bust each other's balls, you'll get used to it," I laughed.

The hustle and bustle of the individual teams worked in perfect unison, as one crew came in another went out and before long the cleaning crew was rolling through room by room as the black and whites taped off the premises. It was a long morning; we discussed the final details in the driveway and a medic mentioned they saw a homeless-looking man racing down the highway on their way here.

"Did you see where he went?" Diego asked.

"Jumped into a green Gran Torino, headed for the desert, I didn't think anything of it till you plucked the brown hair sample," she answered.

"Right, run that sample, see if we get a match. We are looking at a possible repeat offender everyone, he's likely had a hand in everything, not just murder so keep a watchful eye on everything that comes in," I announced to the crew.

"If it's not the same guy we have a copycat on our hands," Diego sighed.

"Let's hope there aren't two maniacs out there," I yawned.

"Wrap it up Hernandez, get the samples to the lab, and go home and get some sleep," I said as I waved him off walking to my car.

As I arrived home my teenage kids were getting up for school, my wife was cooking breakfast burritos and the dog was leaping over me sniffing the odors that I carried home from the crime scene.

"Morning, Honey," I yawned as I took a sip from Lilly's coffee.

"You look terrible," she kissed my cheek as I squeezed a fist full of her ass.

"Another murder…" I sighed as I sat at the breakfast bar on a tall stool.

"Who was it?" Her eyes were big and full of worry.

"Mrs. Garcia…" I whispered.

"Carter's old teacher?" she questioned.

"That's the one," I replied.

I sipped softly at the coffee as I gathered my thoughts of the hours gone by. My kids raced down the stairs attracted by the whiffs of bacon and warm tortillas that flooded the stairwell.

"Did you just get home Dad?" asked Carter.

"Big night bud. You need me to pick you up from practice this afternoon?" I queried.

"I'll text you; I'll try to catch a ride with one of the guys," he replied as he rolled a burrito.

"I'm off for a shower and bed. Goodnight family," I dragged myself up the stairs into the bathroom and ran the shower.

My clothes were heaped in a corner on the floor and my gun sat on the basin. I heard the front door slam as my kids left to catch the bus for school. I stood naked in front of the mirror as I allowed the room to fill with clouds of steam. I heard Lilly's gentle footsteps climb the stairs and I began to tug at my already engorged cock. She often snuck in for a pounding once the kids were gone.

"Detective?" She whispered with her sultry voice.

I turned to the door as the handle twisted and slowly opened. She stood there in all her glory with her breasts exposed, blouse unbuttoned down to her navel, and her long wispy curls tickling her nipples.

I rubbed myself faster as I swelled to my full capacity at the sight of her, she lifted her skirt and to my pleasantry, she had no underwear on, just her smooth waxed pussy as she rubbed her clit, fingers moist and juicy as she plunged them inside herself.

I let go of my cock and moved toward her, unzipping her loose-fitting skirt, and ripping the remaining buttons open from her blouse.

"I guess you want some of this?" I chuckled. Her hands were already stroking me, and I could feel her juices lubricating me as she began to rub herself on my stiffness.

She took my length in her mouth and flicked her tongue gently against me. I was so built up I pulled her away and picked her up, stepped over the bath, and sat her on top of me under the steamy rain the shower sent down on us.

I filled her up with my cock, a little too much as usual but she took control and bounced her perfectly round ass up and down me.

She gasped as she began to slow and did that cute little circular motion she does when she's almost ready to cum. I stood up and picked her up, she threw her legs around me, and I pounded her hard against the wall, she came first but I wasn't done with her, I was gonna fill her up till there was no room left.

My wife was a team player and she bent over while I slammed her from behind, she was dripping now and had shut off the shower, she wanted to feel everything I had to give her. I exploded inside her, and she came again. She pulled away and knelt in front of me and begun sucking every tiny glob she could squeeze from me.

I stroked her hair as she kept her pace swallowing me inch by inch, I was still rock hard, and I throbbed in her mouth as she gobbled on me greedily. I was in a state of euphoria, and I came again filling her mouth with my white load.

She swallowed everything, licking me clean. She turned the shower on again and I began to clean her from behind, her pussy was swelling and warm from the hard pounding I'd given her, but she still raked her body against my fingers as they gently brushed her clit, I thrust 2 fingers inside and with my other hand I circled her clit, she fought against me, but she was weak and ready to cum again. She spun herself around and I dropped to my knees, I took her in my mouth and lashed my tongue over her till I felt her sweet nectar flood my mouth.

She collapsed into me like a puddle, her breathing heavy as she tried to compose herself. Our bodies plugged the bath and water rained down on us once more as we soaked in our bodily fluids as they mixed with the water.

Her face was tired, like my body.

"Take the day off and come to bed with me," I suggested.

"aren't you due back in at noon?" she said with shakiness in her voice.

I sighed... "Yes," I muttered.

"Get some sleep, I'll drop by the station with some dinners," she smiled as she pulled herself from the tub and dried herself off.

"Don't worry about the kids, I'll grab them from practice," she added as she dried her tight curls.

"You're amazing, Lilly. I don't tell you that enough," I smiled at her.

"Only deserving of an equally amazing man," she smiled softly.

Lilly and I were next-door neighbors as kids. Our windows looked into each other's and as teens I watched her cry over cheerleaders teasing her about her beautiful red hair, we would talk through the windows for hours until she stopped sobbing. There was no crushing just a great friendship and then one day I decided I couldn't live my life without those window conversations. Window conversations that suddenly turned to pillow talk, and pillow talk that in turn consumed me completely.

We got married the same year I finished at the Tempe Police Academy, she was pregnant, and we were fumbling our way through life, she became a hairdresser and we scraped together enough money to open her a shop. We blinked our way through successes, promotions, and struggles, and most of all parenthood. Now we wake up to two almost fully grown adult children, a thriving salon and I'm drowning as a detective.

To say we planned it this way would be a harsh misjudgment, we stumbled every step of the way. We struggled to pay school fees, we barely made lease payments on time and there were times when we were eating at Lilly's moms to get us through a bad month.

But every obstacle brought me strength, it gave me drive and that's when I started digging through open cold cases and earned myself my position. I wasn't sitting on my ass like my last 5 partners. I was motivated to do better, to be a better father, and give my kids opportunities.

CLINT

This guy smelt like toxic waste, even worse than that homeless guy I had disposed of before I picked up the shmuck. I was gonna have to scrub the interior with bleach. He wasn't shy about touching either, he tampered with the radio and mocked my music. I pretended to like his rock channel, so he'd calm his wired ass down.

The guy's eyes had that wild bulging effect, his teeth were chattering noisily, and he wouldn't stop fidgeting. His leg kept shaking and I wondered if he knew he was even doing it. He was a good target, a guy like this nobody would miss, you'd be lucky if anyone even noticed him missing till his bones showed up on a development site.

His hair was slick and oily, it hadn't been washed in weeks, his green trench coat had brown stains all over it and he carried a woman's black leather well-worn backpack. It looked heavy and every so often on a fast turn you could hear the clanging of glass knocking together. I assumed beer bottles.

"So, you know where you're headed pal?" I queried curious to hear his response.

"Just out to see our great state in the cheapest way possible." He snickered.

"Oh?" I questioned.

"By hitching free rides every direction, I go." His smiled widened and the fluffy plaque on his teeth beamed out at me like headlights on a road train.

I didn't respond. His comment was offensive and premeditated. The only reason a guy like this would say something insensitive like that is to get a rise from someone. I was the wrong someone to admit you're a lowlife deadbeat to. Specially to imply you were happy to use my fuel, my car and tinker with my radio and not pay your way. This was going to be a long ride; we were miles away from the stack. The big drop I hurled bodies over.

I often wondered if anyone was still alive down there, it was a steep incline, impossible to climb out of and disguised by a hilly rock mound making it look as though the top didn't drop down, a canyon that had no business being there. This moron next to me was snoring, that snore vibrated the damn windows and shook me from my place of euphoric imagination. I was starving, I hadn't eaten all day and the car needed to be filled up, so I smacked Wade on the chest and frightened him as he woke from the impact.

"Hahaha... sorry there, bud."

"What did you do that for?" He stuttered.

" We're gonna pull in somewhere and get some gas and food, I haven't eaten in a while," I announced.

"Oh good, I'm starving," He nodded.

It was a long few miles till we spotted a Walmart, bed bath and beyond with a gas station and pulled into the parking lot. The car jolted to a sudden stop as I slammed on the break hard, inches from the van parked in front of me.

"Woah! Watch it," scowled Wade.

"Sorry, pal." I snickered.

"STOP. CALLING. ME. PAL." He yelled. His voice vibrated my windows some more, the scent of his breath pierced my nasal cavity like a dead corpse that had rotted in the deserts bleeding sunlight for weeks.

Ahh the nostalgia stirred the excited butterflies in my stomach.

"Sorry, Bud. Let's go grab a bite. My treat," I punched him in the shoulder playfully but intendedly hard.

He seemed elated to me offering to buy him food. It was my guess that he had no money anyway.

"Fine, let's go, Bud," He groaned.

His mood was sour, I watched him glance about curiously as if he were looking for an opportunity to do something edgy, likely steal. I got to the counter and Wade stood back so I took the liberty of ordering us burgers and fries with some large shakes. Wade was sat at a table across from an elderly couple who had not invited him to join them. The lady looked uneasy and was covering her nose trying to avoid his scent as her husband began to rush through his food a little faster than before.

"What's that?' Wade asked as he pointed to an onion ring.

"Onion rings," replied the elderly man.

Wade didn't wait for an invitation and snatched one from the plate.

"Ughh, sorry about my friend here," I laughed as I shoved the tray of food in front of Wade.

"No troubles," smiled the old man.

The old lady stood up beside me and whispered into my ear with her sweet squeaky voice.

"Be careful of the company you keep..." she advised.

Little did she know it was likely my company that was far more sinister to keep. She collected her rubbish and hurried her husband as Wade rushed through his food, he was halfway done with his burger when I got to sit down, and his eyes followed that little old couple as they pondered through the store.

"Wade," I snapped wavering my hand in front of his face.

"What?" he asked, his eyes still focused.

"You have sauce on your cheek," I said shaking my head knowing I wasn't going to be able to steer his gaze.

He scoffed his fries and sunk his drink in record timing and began to wander throughout the store. I sat and finished my food slowly as I followed him with my eyes to see where he was going.

His stench wafted offensively through the store making him easy to track. I sat for a short while enjoying my food, the kids in front of me were tossing french fries at one another. Their parents scowling at one another in argument over what sheets to buy.

Then a chip landed in my drink, composing myself wasn't the hard part, it was restraining myself from pouring the drink over the little rots head.

I took a walk to put distance between myself and disruptive family pacing the aisles from cushions to duvets, duvets to sheets, and sheets to bed displays. Through the shelving I could see the section was clear, but I could smell the wretched odor that was Wade's pungent aroma.

The silent murmurs of choking and droplets hitting the floor as if there were a leak in the roof. He was being his usually unusual self. I observed from the shelving before making my presence known. I wanted to see what this creep was really up to. I moved to the other end of the aisle closer to the display bed he was fluffing cushions in.

He was tucking the elderly couple into bed. Their hands covered their eyes and drops of blood trickled down their elbows from the smaller than small double bed. That's the sound I heard. Blood hitting the floor.

Wade looked like a kid in a candy store as he retrieved a jar from his bag and dropped the eyeballs inside. The bodies were gagged, assuming there was still life in them, but then he plucked their tongues out through an open incision in their throats.

I was the enthralled, I knew I had a way about me. I knew I wasn't all right, but I wasn't stupid or messy with my fetishes. I kept a composure about myself. Wade was out in the open in bed bath and beyond dissecting little old people.

The giggling of those pesky little shits got closer, the dads disgruntled deep voice echoed through the large store and Wade nervously begun packing his souvenirs away, he wiped his hands on the sheets and sprung to his feet, bag slung over his back and hands in his pockets.

As he brushed past the father of the kids, I could see his immediate offense to Wade's specialty bouquet. His nose stifled and he rubbed it aggressively.

Wade kept walking quickly and the kids began to jump from one display bed to another. The pure joy on their faces was hard to walk away from, I had to see this unfold. It was thrilling as fuck!

The little girl pounced first to the bed closest to the back wall and then to the bed where Wade had been working. She landed clumsily amongst the sheets, but wade had covered the bodies.

"Oh no!" She cried.

"What?" The older boy asked.

She giggled, likely at the thought of other kids also playing in the beds.

Excited for more, she flung back the sheets and uncovered the elderly couple as she sat between them.

Screams bellowed out through the store and the boy raced for his father, the mother dropped the sheets and charged to examine the commotion.

More screams ensued, the blood had swelled into a pool on the display carpet, the mother had slipped as she tried to retrieve her daughter and I was bursting at the seams trying not to choke on my laughter. Wade had done it. I felt I could tolerate the smelly shit a little more after that.

The father dialed 911 and the store began to lockdown as staff shuffled like ants out of line in utter madness. I snuck away slowly trying to go unnoticed. As the store evacuated, sirens began to hurl into the parking lot. I stepped out through the doors before I could be trapped inside, and Wade was leaning against the passenger door.

"What's all the commotion?" he sighed lightly with a wide grin on his face.

"Bunch of kids stumbled upon some bodies," I smiled wickedly.

Wade glanced at me trying to work out my smile but executed a quick escape by trying to open the car door. I popped the lock and jumped into the car. Wade soon followed and just as the police tried to shut down the exit.

The mother of the children came running from the store to meet the police, she was soaked in blood from slipping on the carpet and yelled directly in mine and Wade's direction as he snickered cheekily, an evil smirk took over his warped smile. The police raced for the car, but we were faster.

I heard my number plate KILR72 screamed over the radio with an accurate description of the green Gran Torino and Wade's description followed.

We blazed down the highway as fast as we could into the sunset. The adrenaline was pumping, I couldn't wait to get my hands dirty with this maggot. He'd never see it coming, as far as he's concerned, I was a meal ticket, a ride to freedom, he had no clue I was preying on him like he had preyed on that elderly couple.

This guy was a verified sicko, I hadn't even seen shit like that in movies. I half expected him to swallow the tongues himself and it gave me creepy vibes to know they weren't even a meter from me swaying in his prized glass jars in his lady bag.

It was tricky keeping myself calm, the excitement was feverish, and I could barely stop my leg from shaking.

WADE

Sirens wailed. Clint pressed his foot harder on the gas and we flew through the darkening roads. Lights became distant and the sounds lessened. My hands were still shoved in my pockets as I kicked around my bag trying to steady it. I hadn't had a chance to tighten the jars properly and I worried my little keepsakes would go flying and alert Clint.

He had this grossly creepy grin on his face, he was full of excitement, wired as hell and I didn't know what to make of it.

"Why so chipper?" I asked.

"Ahhh pal, I just love the thrill of being chased," he blabbered.

"Oh, is that right?" my eyes deceived me as they lit up exhilarated and ready for the challenge.

If it's a chase he loves I'm sure I could deliver. He doesn't have to go out immediately. I flicked my ratty hair to one side and leaned my elbow on the door as Clint raised the volume of the music.

Ugh, more oldies. This time Elvis, I could vomit.

The music was frying what remaining brain cells I had, I tried to block it out as best I could, but the cactus scenery wasn't exactly sensational. So, I lay my head back and went to my happy place and reminisced about the sweet sounds of that tragic geriatric couple, they never saw it coming. I appeared in front of them like a ghost and in an instant, I simultaneously tore through their voice boxes with one wave of my knife, they had taken their final breaths, their blood gushing to the floor, the lady dropped first, then the husband.

That last breath was always exhilarating, knowing I had the power to cease somebodies' existence, what a responsibility, what a treat. I feasted on it like a banshee to a scream.

I smelt the fear as life trickled from their eyes and their existence rolled back into their skulls never to come back. I'd set to work organizing a beautiful stage for all to lay eyes upon, the scene was magnificent.

Thankfully they were small, it was easier to lift them into the bed as I fumbled about with the duvet cover.

Clint kept hitting potholes in the road and disrupting my moment of reflection.

"Take it easy, man!" I growled in an annoyed tone.

"Sorry, pal," he chuckled.

We kept driving, but not in straight lines, we were winding and taking odd turns. I wasn't too familiar with Arizona, but the road signs all begun to repeat themselves and we'd stopped at several gas stations, we were going around in circles, and I started to wonder why.

Clint seemed like a pretty normal kind of a guy, great car, had his hair cut, which is more than I could say for myself. He didn't talk about himself like some folks do, he had a zen about him that was oddly calming. I didn't feel especially drawn to him in the way that I wanted to cut him down the middle, at least not right away. If not for his hideous taste in music I could tolerate this guy a lot longer. Granted, he was overly friendly. Calling me 'pal' and 'bud' were getting on my nerves. Maybe I would string him up and bleed him after all.

We'd successfully averted the sirens and it was easier to relax now. I steadied the jars between my legs as best I could, but it was difficult to cover the sound of sloshing and clanging.

"Ya know pal, I couldn't help but notice you admiring the beds back there," He grinned, slowly taking his eyes away from the road as he lured me in for a reaction.

Fuck, he'd seen me.

"What about it?" I muttered, regretting all pleasantries I had just pondered.

"I'm not much of an on-the-spot kinda guy, pal... I like to watch my prey REAL CLOSE," his eyes lit up and the car began to swerve. He didn't take his eyes from me.

"Prey?" I questioned as I gripped his hand helping to correct the steering wheel.

"Get your hands off me..." he scowled.

"I know what you are, pal... you're a lot like me, the only difference is, I'm the baddest motherfucker in this car..." He snickered as he slammed his foot into the accelerator, the force threw me back into my chair.

My forehead started to sweat, and I quietly tried to reach for the knife in my bag. Clint knew what I was and how I operated. I had gravely underestimated him.

I reached for the knife and touched the tip of the handle when he saw me, he slammed on the brakes again, harder and I'm tossed into the front dash. I hadn't worried about a seatbelt and my body found itself in a messy fetal position.

"You're fucked now, pal," Clint smiled as he put the car into a parked position. He jumped out and ripped me from the car throwing me into the dirt.

I fought back, but for every hit I landed, Clint landed two more. He was built like a marine, his fists delivered blows to my ribs and face and soon I felt swelling in my eyes as the force restricted my vision.

He tore the knife from my hand as he stepped on my wrist to disarm me.

"You won't be needing this. Did you think I was gonna let YOU make ME a victim?" he laughed insultingly.

I tried to respond, it was in my nature to have the last word, but I was frozen and the only thing that came from my mouth was blood.

"You stinky son of a bitch, I knew there was something about you I HAD to have in my trophy case," he smiled.

I tried to pull myself up from the ground, stones embedded in my knees. I knew my only way out was to beg, if I wanted to see another day, I had to work this fool.

"Please Clint, just let me go. I won't bother you. I could even help you. You're like me? Imagine what we could do together?" I pleaded.

Clint gave it thought, but not seriously. His response was to plunge his fists right back into my ribs, followed by his cruel gasping laugh.

"that's what I like, beg some more. Little bitch." He spat at me as I lay in the dry dirt as a heap of defeat.

My response was weak and somber. I wanted to fight, but I had none left in me.

He grabbed the knife and sunk the blade right into my chest. My entire world began to turn black…

DETECTIVE WESTWOOD

Six very short hours of sleep was all I could muster before I had to haul my ass back into the station, and I was exceedingly later than I was meant to be. It was buzzing at the station and a lot more than usual for 4 pm.

"Ahh, look what the cat dragged in!" Hernandez teased. He pushed back his chair and strung his arms behind his head and cackled.

"Relax Hernandez, Westwood's been pulling double shifts since you were in diapers," Stevens chimed in my defense slapping me on the shoulder as she placed a hot coffee in my hand.

"Maybe not that old," I chuckled.

"What's the updates for today," I asked the room as I sipped back my coffee.

"Argh, still haven't got eyes on the suspect," Hernandez snuffed.

"DNA? Prints? We gotta have something on this guy?" I groaned.

"Yes, sir. We have a long brown hair, not the teachers.

"Any tissue on it?" I questioned.

"Nothing, sir," Stevens replied.

"Except for the Medics reporting that hitchhiker rushing into a green Gran Torino heading north. Not many folks head out of town at dawn on a weekday," Hernandez urged.

"it's not enough without plates Diego," I sighed.

"Couldn't hurt to put a call out in surrounding counties," he pressed.

"Did they get a description of the person entering the vehicle?" I enquired.

"Male, sir," He sighed.

"c'mon partner. We're off to the morgue," I pulled his seat forward almost ejecting him onto the floor.

"Why the morgue?" He asked as he caught up with me.

"We need to know exactly what we are dealing with," I hummed.

We arrived at the morgue and were greeted by Dr. Chambers who showed us into the room with the body and revised the report as I peered over his shoulder.

"Anything on the toxicology?" I asked.

"Methamphetamine residue in the left nasal cavity," he croaked.

"No way?" I leaped.

"You knew this woman?" he asked.

"Elena Garcia, she's a teacher at my kids' school," I mumbled.

"Do you wanna know every detail?" The Dr. asked.

"More of a need to know..." I stammered as I observed the mangled fingertips.

"3 Acrylic nails pulled from the nail beds, partial scalping on the left anterior side, right canine incisor forcefully removed, maxillary right canine removed, maxillary incisor chipped, mandibular right incisor also chipped, multiple bruising sites over the gums with loose flesh apparent," He explained it all slowly and animated as he pointed out each point of offense.

"Shall I continue?" he asked as Hernandez swallowed hard.

"There's more?" He gulped.

"A great deal more..." Chambers sighed.

"Give him a breather, we don't often see this stuff in our neck of the woods," I nodded to the Dr.

Diego paced the floor gazing sadly at poor Elena, she was barely recognizable now. The sheet over her hid the monstrous deeds this wandering savage had inflicted on her.

"Okay, go on," Diego nodded.

"Thoracic Vertebrae 1 to 4 shattered with a foreign object, catastrophic punctures to both lungs, blood filled the pleural space, she likely died at this point," Dr. Chambers sighed softly as his eyes left the report to observe my expression.

If I had a mirror, I'd say I was green, I'd heard far fewer horrors that motivated me to do my job, but this was the worst of it. What kind of sick bastard could do all these vile things.

"that's the brunt of it, Westwood. I can hand this over to you now if you like?" Dr. Chambers offered me the clipboard.

"I'd appreciate that, thank you again for your time Dr." I grabbed the clipboard and spun Diego toward the door.

"You alright?" I asked.

We barely made it outside and he was vomiting all over the garden.

"We're gonna catch that motherfucker!" he scowled as he wiped off his face.

"We'll get him," I agreed.

My cell phone buzzed loudly.

"Stevens?" I answered.

"Double homicide 30mins from here at Bed, Bath and Beyond," she growled into the phone.

"Got an MO?"

"Elderly couple gagged in a display bed, had their tongues and eyes torn out," she swallowed loudly.

"That's gotta be our guy," I gasped.

Hernandez leaped into the driver's seat of the car and turned on the sirens as I received more details from Stevens.

"Gran Torino," I muttered to him as the phone call continued.

"Green?" he asked.

"With silver stripes," I added.

"We got plates on that Stevens?" I asked.

"K-I-L-R-7-2," She relayed.

"Well, that wasn't accidental," Diego added.

"There are two suspects in the vehicle, considered to be highly dangerous and armed, back up is minutes behind you, approach with caution. They can't be too far away," Stevens hung up the phone and I checked my gun ready to use it.

"No hesitations Diego," I glared at him as his eyes bulged.

"None, I'm ready!" he smiled.

Calls kept coming through the radio with information.

"I'm gonna run an NCIC," I noted to Diego.

"Haven't they already done that?" Diego glared.

"Not that they've relayed to me," I scowled in humor.

"Useless deputies..." Diego laughed.

Diego began to call in to check the results.

"Your plates come back as a 1972 green Ford Gran Torino, registered to a Clint Kelly of 1342 Cactus Lane, Tempe Arizona," the dispatch officer announced.

"10-4," Diego responded.

Diego took in a deep breath and hit the gas harder trying to make up for lost time.

It wasn't long till we came upon fresh skid marks, the smell of burnt rubber still lingering in the air. They carried on for many feet past optical vision, they wound around a bend and cut off on a dirt trail with dry dusty dirt tossed out of place. I knew these had to be our guys.

Instead of waiting for backup Diego blazed the cruiser through the dirt and followed the tire marks up a dusty cactus-filled hill that looked out over a small out-of-place canyon, it was deep but hardly visible as night began to creep in.

In the distance, a silhouette could be seen from the light of the cars. A stocky man of about 5'11 was dragging what seemed to be a body. Diego recklessly launched himself from the car, and cocked his gun.

"Hernandez! NO!" I shouted.

He turned back to me, but the suspect heard my cries, dropped the body, and ran after Hernandez.

I readied my gun in what felt like slow motion and climbed down from the car onto the ground. But there was no retaliation firing and Diego's gun was spitting blanks. The idiot had been so excited he loaded a blank mag.

The guy quickly noticed and took his opportunity, he ran up behind Hernandez, punched him in the back of the head, immediately knocking him to the ground.

I was frozen, I couldn't move. Flashes of my life flickered through my mind, the birth of my kids, my wedding. Lilly raced through my mind, I felt like running away for the first time in my career that I had worked so hard for. The threat of imminent danger had shaken me.

Diego's cries were muffled through my memories and then I saw the knife plunged into his jugular vein deep into his neck. Blood sprayed over who I could only assume to be Clint Kelly.

Clint looked up, leaving the knife in Diego's neck. He came towards me, sighting my hesitation. Wearing a grin from ear to ear that projected the devil himself.

"Any last words pig?" he snickered.

"Why?" I stammered. He froze as he considered my question.

Clint stopped in his tracks and gave me a puzzled look.

"Why not?" Clint smiled.

"Are you the one who tortured Elena Garcia? And the elderly couple at Bed, Bath & Beyond?" I scowled.

"Me? Sorry, not my style,"

"But that heap of shit, probably..." He pointed to the direction of the first body.

"So, why not walk away the hero?" I questioned.

"Hero? I wasn't born to be the hero," he chuffed.

"Maybe not, but you can do the right thing for once in your life," I pressed trying to appeal to his better nature. Even if he wasn't the guy responsible, he was now the guy who had just murdered my partner in cold blood.

Clint's bushy brows raised, and I couldn't tell if it was anger or thought. He lowered his guard. He knew he could get away with this, he just had to take me out. He'd get away, Diego moved too fast, we hadn't notified back up of our location. We were on our own.

"What's your name, son?" I asked.

"Clint…" he hesitated.

"Clint Kelly?" I questioned.

"Yes, sir," he nodded.

"I'm Detective Charles Westwood. Now we can walk away from this and nobody else has to get hurt, we can appeal for a lighter sentence. You just killed a seriously twisted serial killer. The jury would take that in your favor," I urged.

The grin returned to Clint's face. He came uncomfortably closer.

"You wanna help me after I just put down your partner? You have no backup detective; I know you cops like to sweet-talk your way into a conviction. Your mine…" he cackled.

I took the safety off my gun as I slid my hand into my back pocket. I knew what was about to happen, but I wouldn't let this sorry son of a bitch take me down the way he took down Diego.

Clint rushed at me; his fists loaded. I pulled the gun and fired a warning shot, he kept coming. He was fast for a big guy, he got to the gun before I could shoot again and gripped me from behind. We scuffled till we were both face to face playing tug of war with the gun, suddenly we hit the ground and dust flew around in mirky clouds that blinded my sight, I had to rely on my sense of feel and the weight of his breath was raining down on me.

I opened my eyes to Clint on top of me, still fighting desperately for the gun. Clint finally released his grip from one hand and plunged it into my face. Opportunity struck and with the weight gone from the gun, I gripped the trigger and squeezed it, blowing a hole through his chest.

He fell to the ground gasping for air as the color left his face and blood begun to drain from his wound. I stood over him and watched the life evade his body as he took his last gasps for air.

Funnily enough, he left the world with a smile on his face. I rushed over to check on Diego, but I already knew I was too late. His body was limp and lifeless.

I walked over to check on the original victim. He had multiple stab wounds, bruising, and a wretched stench about him.

Lastly, I walked back to the cruiser and radioed in for backup and EMS to come to the scene.

Three casualties and I couldn't help but wonder where he was dragging the body to before we interrupted him.

"Dispatch, I need all available units to my location to start a search, I have three confirmed dead, one officer down and I got a hunch we're gonna solve a lot of cold cases. I also think we have our guy from the Bed, Bath & Beyond, DOA," I ordered.

"10-4, sending all units," Stevens replied.

The headlights from the cars beamed over the canyon and I could make out what appeared to be people's belongings.

I'm getting too old for this shit. I kicked the dirt and sat patiently waiting for back up beside Diego.

"We got them, buddy," tears pooled in my eyes as I stroked the hair off his face and tried to clean away the blood as best I could.

My phone rang and Lilly's name flashed over the screen.

I answered but I was silent, she could only hear my pain.

"Charles?" she begged.

"I'm okay Lil," I sobbed.

"Diego?" she asked.

"No..." I stammered.

I could hear Callie in the background wailing.

"Where are you?" I asked.

"I brought dinner to the station; Callie came to see Diego. We heard what happened over the radio." Her voice was heavy.

"I'm sorry, Lil. It all just happened too fast..." I hung up the phone as crews rolled into my location.

The End.

A KLLER RIDE

U. J. Garland

CPSIA information can be obtained
at www.ICGtesting.com
Printed in the USA
LVHW032253140921
697834LV00012B/1278